DON'T STAND
SO CLOSE
TO ME

DON'T STAND SO CLOSE TO ME

Eric Walters

ORCA BOOK PUBLISHERS

Copyright © Eric Walters 2020

Published in Canada and the United States in 2020 by Orca Book Publishers.
orcabook.com

Library and Archives Canada Cataloguing in Publication
Title: Don't stand so close to me / Eric Walters.
Other titles: Do not stand so close to me
Names: Walters, Eric, 1957– author.
Identifiers: Canadiana (print) 20200252410 | Canadiana (ebook) 20200252445 |
ISBN 9781459827875 (softcover) | ISBN 9781459827882 (PDF) |
ISBN 9781459827899 (EPUB)
Classification: LCC PS8595.A598 D66 2020 | DDC jc813/.54—DC23

Library of Congress Control Number: 2020938515

Summary: In this novel for middle readers, 13-year-old Quinn and her
friends try to adjust to life during the COVID-19 pandemic.

Orca Book Publishers is committed to reducing the consumption of
nonrenewable resources in the making of our books. We make every
effort to use materials that support a sustainable future.

Orca Book Publishers gratefully acknowledges the support for its
publishing programs provided by the following agencies: the Government of
Canada, the Canada Council for the Arts and the Province of British Columbia
through the BC Arts Council and the Book Publishing Tax Credit.

Typeset by Ella Collier
Cover design by Rachel Page
Cover artwork by Gettyimages.ca/the_burtons
and Gettyimages.ca/molotovcoketail

Printed and bound in Canada.

23 22 21 20 • 1 2 3 4

For my grandchildren — Quinn, Isaac and Reese —
and the future they will help to create.

Chapter One

"Isaac, could you please pay at least a *little* attention?" Jenna asked.

Isaac looked up from his phone. "Believe me, I'm paying as little attention as I can," he said.

Reese and I tried hard not to laugh, but it was impossible. Isaac just didn't care.

"Do you have to encourage him, Quinn?" Jenna said, frowning at me. She turned to Isaac. "Why are you even here if you don't want to take any of this seriously?"

"I have no choice," said Isaac. He turned to Miss Fernandez, who was sitting in the corner of the classroom, reading a book. "Right?"

"Correct," replied Miss Fernandez, looking up.

"The president of the student council must attend all planning meetings."

"Bet you didn't know that when you ran for president," Jenna said.

"I'm constantly amazed by what I didn't know," Isaac replied. "I'm starting to wish you'd won the election."

Jenna shot him a dirty look. Isaac was president and she was vice-president. The person who came in second was automatically appointed vice-president.

Jenna had *really* wanted to be president. She had built a committee to help her, created a formal platform of promises and put up all sorts of fancy signs throughout the school.

Isaac had put up a few signs too. We'd even helped make them. But his said things like *Vote for Isaac — You Could Do Worse* and *Isaac — The Only A's I Get Are in My Name*. He'd run for school president as a joke. He'd never thought he could actually win. But I had. Things like that just happened to Isaac. It didn't hurt that he was on all the school sports teams and was liked by everybody. Even when he got into trouble—which was often—it was for harmless or goofy reasons. It even seemed like

Mrs. Reynolds, our principal, felt bad when she had to punish him.

Isaac was one of my best friends, but Jenna was too. I didn't like them fighting. I didn't like *anybody* fighting. It made me feel anxious.

"Isaac, can we get back to business?" I asked.

"For you, Quinny, I will attempt to focus." He put his phone in his pocket.

I'd known Isaac forever—literally. We lived next door to each other and were born a month apart. He was always over at my house or I was at his.

"We only have a few weeks left to plan the spring dance," Jenna said.

"You need a venue and some music," Isaac said. "I'm assuming the gym is where this is happening. How hard can the rest be?"

"Actually, we have to arrange refreshments, chaperones, agree on a theme, decorate, create a playlist—"

"And get the songs on that playlist approved," Miss Fernandez chimed in.

"Get the playlist approved, book a DJ and—"

"I could be the DJ!" Isaac exclaimed.

Reese and I laughed again.

"And why is that funny?" Isaac asked. "I love music."

"How about if I take this one?" Reese said to me. "Isaac, your musical taste is all rap, heavy metal and classic rock."

"And your point?"

"A dance generally involves dancing," Reese explained. "That would be pretty hard to do with the kind of songs you like."

"Hmmm. Uh, Miss Fernandez? Follow-up question," said Isaac. "Do I actually have to go to this dance?"

"Yes, Isaac," Miss Fernandez said with a sigh. "As the student council president, you are definitely expected to attend."

Isaac thought for a moment. "Well then, I will still volunteer to be the DJ. Someone else can figure out the playlist, and I'll just be my usual charming and funny self."

Jenna tapped her clipboard. "Okay, fine. But can we get back to this list? We only have six weeks to get all of this organized."

"Six weeks is almost six weeks more than we need," said Isaac. "You worry too much."

"Well, next week is spring break," Jenna said. "And some of us won't be around. Aren't you going to Mexico, Quinn?"

"We were planning to," I replied, "but our trip has been, um, postponed." My father was a doctor, and the hospital staff had recently been told they had to postpone any upcoming vacation plans.

"Well, I'm going south," Isaac said.

"You are?" I asked. I was surprised I hadn't heard anything about that.

"Well, the south part of town. I got friends who live there." Isaac, always the joker.

"You're going someplace, right, Jenna?" Reese asked.

Jenna nodded. "We're going to visit my aunt and uncle in California for a few days. My cousin is getting married, and it's a big family reunion. We leave tomorrow morning."

"Wait. You're skipping a day of school?" Isaac asked. "I think that is *inappropriate*." He was doing a perfect imitation of our principal. "School is *very* important, young lady!"

Everybody, including Miss Fernandez, laughed.

Just then Mrs. Reynolds appeared at the

classroom doorway. Everybody instantly stopped laughing. I was pretty sure we were all afraid she'd overheard.

"Good afternoon, Mrs. Reynolds," Isaac sang out. "Always a pleasure to see you."

Mrs. Reynolds narrowed her eyes, and Isaac dropped his to his desk. Isaac's mother was the police chief in our town, but she was nowhere near as scary as Mrs. Reynolds.

"Miss Fernandez, may I speak to you for a moment?" she asked.

Miss Fernandez stood up, and they both went into the hall.

"What do you think that's about?" Reese asked.

"Miss Fernandez is in *trouble*," Isaac said. "I know that look!"

"I highly doubt that, Isaac," I replied. Geez, the guy would say anything for a laugh.

But when Miss Fernandez came back into the room, she *did* look like she had gotten into trouble.

"That seemed serious," Isaac commented.

"It was. It is."

"What's going on?" I asked.

"Mrs. Reynolds is calling an assembly so everyone can hear the details. But I can tell you that it involves spring break."

"It better not be canceled!" Isaac exclaimed.

Miss Fernandez looked a bit uncomfortable when she replied. "No, it's not canceled," she said.

What the heck was going on?

Chapter Two

It wasn't long after lunch that we were brought into the gym. Class by class, all four hundred of us. As eighth graders, we got the benches in the back. The sevens were on the floor in front of us, the sixes in front of them and then the fives right in front of the stage.

I watched a couple of fifth graders settling onto the gym floor. They looked so young. It was hard to imagine I was ever that small. The start of fifth grade seemed like a lifetime ago. Now we were at the other end of middle school. In three months our time here would be over, and we would all be going off in different directions and to different high schools. A few eighth graders were even moving away after the school year ended.

Mrs. Reynolds came onto the stage, followed by our vice-principal and then Isaac and Jenna. As student council president and vice-president, they typically sat up there during assemblies. Isaac waved at the crowd as he crossed the stage. There was nothing he liked better than an audience.

Mrs. Reynolds came to the podium. Teachers all over the gym shushed their classes, and soon there was silence.

"Good afternoon, everyone," she began. "I want to thank you for your quiet and orderly entrance to this emergency assembly."

Emergency? What was the emergency? I hated emergencies. I hated anything I couldn't predict. But I suspected I knew what this might be about.

"As you are all aware, there has been growing concern about the spread of a virus that causes a disease known as COVID-19."

I knew all about this virus. It had become a big part of family discussions at dinner. It was also the reason our vacation had been canceled. I also knew that many of the kids didn't seem to know much about it. Mrs. Reynolds talked about health officers and government guidelines. Finally she mentioned spring break.

"We have made some changes to the upcoming spring-break schedule."

The room was suddenly filled with the mumbling of conversation as everyone tried to guess what came next. Mrs. Reynolds stopped talking and waited. She raised a hand, and the gym went silent again.

"As you know, tomorrow was meant to be our last day of school before the break. However, this year the break will start one day early. There will be no school tomorrow."

A gigantic cheer went up from the students. We were getting an extra day off!

Mrs. Reynolds raised her hand again, and the teachers worked to quiet their classes.

"Everybody, listen!" Miss Fernandez said. "This is important."

It got quiet again.

"As part of district plans to create more of what they're calling *social* or *physical distancing,* all schools in the area will be closed for three weeks instead of just one."

The gym erupted in cheers again. Three weeks off! The principal signaled for silence once more.

"Classes are scheduled to begin again at the beginning of April. Your teachers are working on a plan to make sure you don't fall behind in your studies."

This time there wasn't cheering but multiple muttered conversations around the gym. I wondered if we were going to get homework to do over the extra-long break.

Mrs. Reynolds continued. "Please remember that things could change. I will keep you and your parents informed of details as they become available."

Her voice sounded shaky. Was she nervous? Standing up there in front of everybody like this would be a little nightmare for me, but it couldn't be the reason for her. The principal didn't *get* nervous, she made *other* people nervous.

"That is all for now. Thank you. Please return to your classes, where your teachers can answer any questions you may have. Have a great break, everyone."

"I didn't see that coming," Reese said as our class filed out of the gym. "Quite a big surprise."

"Yeah," I said.

But it was not a big surprise for me. My father had been filling us in on all sorts of things that were being planned or talked about. Most of it hadn't seemed real, like closing down schools and even businesses. It wasn't that I hadn't believed him, but it hadn't seemed like something that would actually happen. Now it was real. He was right, and I wished he was wrong.

We got back to class and took our seats.

"Okay," Miss Fernandez said. "Just to recap. We will be starting our break one day early and will not be returning to school for three full weeks. Questions?"

Hands shot up around the room.

"Why are they doing this?" Sasha asked.

"You heard Mrs. Reynolds mention the terms *physical* or *social distancing*? What that means is keeping people apart so they can't pass on the virus to others if they have it or get it from someone else if they don't."

"Does anybody even know someone who has it?" Sasha asked.

"I don't know if there's anyone in our town, but

I do know there are cases across our country. And in *every* country."

"Quinn, your father is a doctor. Is he seeing anybody that has the virus?" Oliver asked.

I had heard my father telling my mother some things, but I wasn't sure what I should repeat. I tried to keep my answer as general as possible.

"There are some cases at the city hospital. My father has treated them."

"What? Are you serious?" said Oliver.

Somebody else jumped in. "My mom says there really aren't that many."

"And that's why we're doing this," Miss Fernandez said. "By closing schools for a longer break, we can make sure the virus doesn't get passed around, and try to keep it from getting out of control."

"I heard it isn't even that bad," Darius said. "It's like the flu."

"It's not like the flu," I said without thinking. Everybody turned toward me. I had no choice but to go on. "People are dying from this."

"Yeah, well, my grandmother died last year after getting the flu," said Sam.

"I'm very sorry for your loss, Sam," Miss Fernandez said, "but I have to agree with Quinn. This is worse than the regular flu."

Just then Isaac burst in the door. "Woo-hoo! Longer break!"

A couple of the guys cheered, but I didn't think Isaac got the big response he'd hoped for. Miss Fernandez motioned for him to zip his mouth and pointed to his seat. As he walked to his desk, he and a few of the guys exchanged low fives and fist bumps.

Sam started talking again. "Maybe they should wait until there are more cases and see what happens."

"That would be bad," Reese said. "They can't wait for exponential growth."

This time everyone turned and stared at Reese. My friend, the math whiz.

"Would you mind explaining what that means to the class, Reese?" Miss Fernandez asked.

"Well, I do love to get all geeky about probability formulas, but the way Quinn explained it to me yesterday is probably easier to understand."

"Quinn? Do you want to give it a try?" Miss Fernandez asked.

I really didn't want to, but it seemed like I had no choice. I took a deep breath. "It might be better if I showed you how my dad explained it to me."

I stood up and walked toward the whiteboard. I picked up a marker and drew a large circle at the top. "Let's say this is Isaac."

"That doesn't look anything like me," he chirped.

"Isaac, stop," said Miss Fernandez. "Quinn, please continue."

I wrote *Isaac* and *COVID-19* in the middle of the circle.

"Let's say Isaac is infected with the virus."

"I'm not."

"But let's say you are." I drew four more circles underneath his circle and wrote a name in each— *Darius*, *Noah*, *Dev* and *Oliver*. Isaac's buddies.

"You just infected these four."

"How did he infect us?" Oliver asked.

"All of you touched his hand when he walked in, so now you have it too."

I wrote *COVID-19* in all four circles. Then I drew smaller circles under each to represent the people living in their houses, five under Darius's name, three under Dev's circle and two under Oliver's and Noah's. We'd all been going to school together for years, so I knew who was in each family.

"And each of you will pass it on to your brothers and sisters and parents." I wrote *COVID-19* in each of the smaller circles.

I kept drawing more and more circles. "And your family members will pass it on to friends, or soccer teammates, or people they work with, or people they meet when they're out shopping." Soon there were so many circles that all the blank space on the board was filled.

"Well done, Quinn," said Miss Fernandez. "As you can see from this great visual, class, one infected person quickly becomes four who become twenty who become seventy. That is exponential growth. Can we get a round of applause for Quinn?"

People clapped as I sat down. I was just relieved to take my seat and get out of the spotlight.

"And what do you think a solution to this type of growth might be?" Miss Fernandez asked.

"Nobody should have any contact with Isaac?" Reese offered.

Everybody, including Isaac, laughed.

"You're laughing, but that's exactly what we need to do. By reducing our contact with each other, the hope is that we will stop this virus from spreading exponentially."

"I still don't really get it," Sam said.

"Let's see if I can explain it another way," said Miss Fernandez. "I'd like to hire one of you to work for me, doing various chores around my house. You'll start after breakfast and work until dinnertime. I'm willing to pay you one dollar for your first day."

"What a rip-off!" Noah yelled.

"But I promise that the next day I'll double your pay. So you'll get two dollars."

"Still no way," Noah said.

"And each day I will continue to double your pay from the day before. Anybody interested in taking me up on my offer now?"

"How long do you want us to work for you?" I asked. I figured I knew where this was going.

"Three weeks."

"I'm in. I'll take the job," I said.

"That's a bad move," said Noah. "You're basically working for nothing!"

"Actually, Noah, Quinn has made a very good decision. I'll show you why."

Miss Fernandez erased all my circle art from the whiteboard and made a grid. There were three rows and seven columns, representing the three weeks. She wrote *$1* in the first grid box, then *$2*, then *$4*. By the end of the first week, *$64* was in the seventh box. In the second week the first grid started with *$128* and went to *$8,192*. The third week began with *$16,384*. Miss Fernandez kept writing. The class got a bit noisy as students started to understand.

"So even though I started by paying Quinn only one dollar, at the end of three weeks, I will be paying her slightly more than *one million dollars* for her work that day. That is exponential growth. Do you all understand what it means now?" Miss Fernandez asked.

"It means I'm definitely going to ask Quinn to marry me," Isaac said.

Some kids gave him the laugh he was after. I gave him a scowl.

"Well, I'm pretty sure Quinn will make another good decision about that," Miss Fernandez said with a smile. "Any more questions?"

Rachel put her hand up. I was a little surprised. She was nice, but hardly ever spoke up in class.

"This physical distancing or whatever is only going to be for a couple of weeks, right?"

"I can't imagine it will last any longer than that," Miss Fernandez said. "But we'll just have to wait and see."

Rachel looked less worried, and I felt better too.

"Now gather up your things. And don't forget to take home some reading material. You're welcome to borrow anything you like," said Miss Fernandez, pointing to the shelves of the class library. "I want you all to have a nice, relaxing break. But not *too* relaxing!"

Chapter Three

We stood at the door, giving each other goodbye hugs. There was a lot of drama going on, but I wasn't totally sure why. It was just three weeks, not forever. While I was hugging people, I couldn't help but think about the circles I'd drawn on the whiteboard. If somebody *did* have the virus already, then a whole bunch of other people were going to be infected now. But I didn't want to be rude. These were my friends.

Reese and I headed across the schoolyard, our backpacks filled with books. We had grabbed as many as we could.

Up ahead Isaac was playing a game of three-on-three with the guys. The game looked like a hybrid of basketball, football and wrestling. Between the shoving and the name calling, you'd have thought they really didn't like each other if you didn't know they were friends. As we got closer, the ball went flying and Noah chased after it.

"Are you walking home with us?" Reese asked Isaac. He usually did, since we all lived so close to each other.

"We're almost finished."

"Two minutes and we're gone," I said.

He turned to his friends. "Is anybody keeping score?"

"I thought *you* were," Darius replied.

"Okay, in that case, how about whoever gets to six points first wins."

Mrs. Reynolds came around the corner of the school. She was always outside for our arrival, lunch and dismissal. She came toward us. I gave Reese a little nudge so she'd notice her.

The boys kept playing. The wrestling component seemed to be the biggest part of their game.

Mrs. Reynolds came up and stood beside us. "What kind of game are they playing?" she asked.

"It's an Isaac original," I replied.

"Excuse me!" she called out. They all stopped. "I'm afraid you gentlemen will have to stop playing now. The directive I received from the district is that students are to leave the school property immediately."

"Couldn't we just—"

She silenced Isaac with a glance. "Immediately."

"Yes, ma'am."

"I wish you all a safe extended break," Mrs. Reynolds said. She turned directly to me. "Quinn, please pass along my thanks to your father for the work he's doing."

"Sure. Of course." It felt weird to be singled out. But I knew my dad would appreciate hearing those kind words.

Mrs. Reynolds left, and Reese and I started to walk home, not waiting for the boys to say their goodbyes. We were only partway across the schoolyard when Isaac caught up to us.

"Whoa. What a day!" he said.

"Yeah, I can't believe what just happened," Reese said. "My parents didn't mention any of this to me." Reese's mother taught at the local high school, and her father was an elementary-school teacher.

"I can," Isaac replied.

"And what makes you so smart?"

"Not smart, but I do listen. I heard my mother on the phone last night with the mayor. She was talking about school closures."

"And you didn't say anything to us?" Reese asked.

"My mother has a gun. I try not to get on her bad side," said Isaac with a wink. "Seriously, though, last night it sounded like just talk. Nothing had been decided."

"Did you know anything, Quinn?" Reese asked.

"Not about the schools closing, but like I said in class, my dad has talked a bit about the virus. It's worse than some people think."

"But not that bad," Reese said.

"My dad says that nobody knows how bad it could get."

"If it means an extra-long holiday, that's not so bad," Isaac said.

"What are you going to do with all that extra time?" I asked.

"Oh, you know. Sleep in, play video games, hang with friends. Maybe create a funny video that goes viral and makes me famous. Mom will be working most of the time, so me alone in the house, unsupervised, is a dream come true."

Isaac's parents had separated a few years back. He joked about loving all the freedom, but I knew it had been hard on him. It still was. His father now lived halfway across the country, and Isaac really missed him. I knew they talked on the phone almost daily, but that was different than living under the same roof.

"What about you two. Any plans?" Isaac asked.

"Some of the same stuff and, of course, reading," I said. I didn't mention the canceled trip to Mexico. Even if we weren't going now, there was no point in rubbing it in.

"We borrowed a *lot* of books," Reese said, twisting so Isaac could see her bulging backpack.

"That many books would get me through the next three years," he said.

"Really?"

"Okay, the next three decades."

We were still laughing when we got to the corner where Reese would keep going straight but Isaac and I would turn. She lived two streets over from us. She gave me a big hug.

"No hug for me?" Isaac asked.

"No way. I heard you were infected," she said with a smile.

"See what you started?" he asked me. "Let me set the record straight. First off, I am, in fact, infected, but it's with joy and happiness. I spread those around in an exponential way. And second, your loss."

"Whatever. Goodbye, Quinn. See ya, Isaac," said Reese.

We walked for a bit in silence and then Isaac asked, "This is why you canceled your trip, isn't it?"

"Yeah. Hospital staff were asked to postpone any trips."

"Thought so. Same for the police department. My mother canceled time off for all officers for the next few weeks. And she told me she wasn't going to be home a lot right now."

"Oh. I didn't know that."

"I think they're being a little paranoid," Isaac said.

"Better safe than sorry."

"Yeah, yeah, and look before you leap, and safety first is safety always, and the grass is always greener on the other side."

I didn't want to get into this discussion. My dad had plenty to say about people who weren't taking this seriously. "I don't think that last saying of yours works."

"It depends on how high the fence is. You could get hurt if you fell."

"Okay, whatever you say. See you later." I started up my driveway.

"See you tomorrow, Quinny," he said. "Three weeks off!" he added, pumping his fist in the air. "Woo-hoo!"

Chapter Four

I was in the kitchen when I heard footsteps. I looked up just as my father came up from the basement.

"Hey, Dad. I didn't know you were home."

"Hey, Q-Cat." He was the only one who called me that. "I got in about twenty minutes ago."

"Oh. I didn't hear you."

"I came in through the garage door and went straight into the basement."

"Why didn't you use the front door?"

"I wanted to be able to change out of my scrubs, put them straight into the washer and have a shower."

"I didn't know you do that after every shift."

"It's just been the last few days."

"Oh." I wasn't sure if that was a good or a bad thing. "Did you hear about schools being closed?"

"Yes. It's all over the news. I think it's a very wise precaution."

I noticed he had several red lines on his face. "What happened to your face?

He put a hand to the bridge of his nose. "Those are just pressure marks from the mask and face shield I have to wear when I see patients."

"You don't usually have those marks."

"I don't usually have to wear PPE—that's short for personal protective equipment—as much as I do now. Hey, you hungry?"

"Depends. Are you making dinner tonight?"

"Yes indeed."

"Is Mom working late tonight?"

"Not too late. She'll be home by six or six thirty. Do you want to help me with dinner?"

"If I help, does that mean I don't have to do any of the cleanup?"

"Sounds fair. Come on, I want this to be a special meal."

- ☺ -

"Please pass the potatoes," my father said.

I took a couple more for myself and passed the bowl down to him. He piled them on beside the meat and asparagus. He had a lot of everything. My father was definitely a meat and potatoes guy.

"You've had quite the appetite the last week or so," my mother commented.

"I'm burning it off. Long days, working harder, running faster. Anyway, how was work today?" he asked. My mother worked for a bank.

"Busy. We had a full staff meeting today, and they're talking about setting us up to work remotely."

"What does that mean?" I asked.

"It means I might start working from home. A lot of what I do could be done by phone or video calls."

"That might be good," my father said.

"It certainly would cut down on the commute. But it will create some real challenges too," she said, turning to me. "But we'll figure it out. So, Quinn, how was *your* day?"

"It was a very normal day until it wasn't. I guess I get a really long spring break now."

"What a shame we had to cancel our trip," my mom said with a sigh.

"Yes, the timing is unfortunate," said my dad. "But this is not the time to be leaving the country. I wouldn't be surprised if some people end up having to cut their trips short."

"Yes, I know you're right," Mom replied. "I just was so looking forward to a little time in the sun. So tell us how your day went."

"It was hard. I'm exhausted."

My father's words surprised me. He was always so positive. He loved being a doctor.

"Things are ramping up," he continued. "We had almost double the cases admitted today than we had yesterday."

"But it's still not too bad, right?" I asked.

"No need for you to worry. I just wish we had more information. There are different opinions about how the virus is spread. We're not even sure just how long it lasts on different types of surfaces."

"Like clothes?" I asked.

"Yes."

"And that's why you came in through the side door, changed your clothes and showered downstairs?"

My father nodded. "But I'm not sure that's enough."

My parents exchanged a long look. "Quinn, we want to let you know something, so there are no surprises," my mother said.

My father nodded. They both knew surprises made me uneasy.

"There is going be a change in our living accommodations," my father said.

"We're moving?"

"No, no, that's not what I mean," he said.

"And it will only be a temporary change," my mother said. "Your father is going to start living in the basement."

"What? Why?"

"To minimize contact with you and your mom. I don't want to risk passing anything on to you. I'll come and go through the side door and eat and sleep downstairs."

My mother reached out and placed a hand on his arm. "Are you *sure* this is necessary?"

"Better safe than sorry."

I smiled slightly. I was remembering that I had just said the same thing to Isaac.

"I need to make sure you two are safe."

"But who's going to make sure *you're* safe?" I asked.

"I'll be careful. I'll wear all the right equipment when I'm working, wash carefully and sanitize everything."

"Quinn," my mother said, "we just have to trust that your father will do everything he can to take care of himself. But we don't want you to worry. Everything is going to be fine. Now, who's ready for a special dessert?"

"I am," my father said, raising his hand. "Unfortunately I think all we have is ice cream."

"All we *had*," my mother said.

She got up, disappeared down the hall and returned with a box that I recognized before I even saw the name on it. McCormick's Bakery. I knew that inside the box would be a pineapple upside down cake—my favorite.

Chapter Five

I heard the sound of a basketball hitting the pavement and thumping against a backboard. I knew it had to be Isaac. I put my shoes on and went outside. Isaac was shooting hoops on his driveway. I grabbed my bike and walked it onto the driveway and across the little grass strip between our houses.

"How's it going?" I asked.

"Day five seems to be as sucky as days two through four," he replied. "Wait, that reminds me."

Isaac picked up a big piece of sidewalk chalk from the driveway and walked onto the road. He made a thick line through four other thick strokes. I didn't understand, and then it came to me. It was a tally of the days that had passed.

"I saw a movie about people in prison. This is what they did to keep track of the days," he explained.

"You're not exactly in a prison."

"Not just prison, but solitary confinement," he said.

"Some people have it a lot worse, you know. At least you have your mother with you. And me living next door."

"I guess you're right. And my prison does have video games, Netflix and all the food I can eat. I'm pretty lucky."

"How's your mom doing?"

"Working a lot, like I guess your dad is. She pops home once in a while but probably just to make sure I'm not getting into trouble."

"What happened to all the amazing things you were going to be doing on break?"

"I don't know. It's different with nobody to hang out with. Physical distancing sucks, and my mom says I'm supposed to stay close to home. You going for a ride?"

"Yes, Reese and I are going to see her grandmother at the Vista Villa Lodge."

"Can I join you?"

"I thought your mother said you were supposed to stay close to home."

"Staying close is a relative term. How far away is it?"

"Maybe fifteen minutes. You sure you want to come?"

"It's better than what I'm doing now. Hang on, I'll get my bike."

— 😊 —

We rode along the bike path. There were lots of people out—walking, riding and jogging. Not just kids or a person or two, but whole families. The paths and parks were busy. It seemed like every swing was being used, and the leash-free areas were full of dogs and their owners.

"It's good to get out and get moving," Isaac said.

"Really good to get away from my parents," Reese said. "They're freaking out."

"Why?"

"They're trying to sort out distance education."

"Why? Do they think we won't be going back to school?" Isaac asked.

"Who knows? But they're trying to learn how to use something called Zoom to talk to their students."

"I know Zoom. It's a platform you can use to talk to lots of people at once," Isaac explained.

"My parents both think it seems like a lot of work to make up for a few lost days of school," Reese said. "They think this will all be over soon."

She was right. It was a lot of work for a few missed days of school. But from what I'd heard, it could be a lot more than a few days. My father wasn't telling us much about what was happening at the hospital, but he was leaving earlier and coming home later. Most nights he wasn't even home by the time I went to bed. I missed our meals together and just hanging out with him and giving him a bedtime hug.

While my father was home less, my mother was home more. The bank had most of the staff working from home if they could. Mom had turned the spare bedroom into a little home office. We had an office in the basement, but because Dad was down there, she couldn't use it.

"How old is your grandmother?" Isaac asked.

"She'll be turning eighty-four in a few weeks."

"I've met her before, right? Doesn't she make those killer ginger cookies?"

"Yes! She used to live over on Chestnut, but it got too hard for her to run her own place. She's had some bad luck."

Reese had told me that her grandma had fallen a couple of times and that she'd left a pot on the stove once and caused a little fire.

"She's gotten a little forgetful," Reese said. "But she's still good."

The building was just up ahead. It was almost new, red brick and seven stories high. There were gardens with flower beds, grass where residents could sit and paths for them to walk on or be pushed along in wheelchairs. I had been here before. It was nice inside too—it reminded me of a Holiday Inn. Reese's grandmother had a unit on the second floor, with a window looking out on the gardens.

We put our bikes off to the side of the front door. Reese grabbed the door and pulled. "It's locked," she said, surprised. "It's never locked."

In the window was a handmade sign.

Effective Immediately — Absolutely NO Visitors

"What does that mean?" Reese asked.

"I think it's pretty obvious," Isaac said. "They're not letting people visit."

"But I want to see my grandmother."

A nurse appeared at the door. She clicked the lock off and opened the door ever so slightly.

"I'm here to see my grandmother, Jennie Ellis."

"Sorry, as of midnight last night, we're closed to visitors as a precaution. We don't want any of the residents to contract the virus."

"But we don't have it," Reese said.

"We can wait outside and Reese can go in alone," I offered.

"Sorry. There are no exceptions."

"My grandmother is all right, isn't she?" Reese asked.

"Everybody is fine. We're in the process of notifying family members about visits being canceled. Again, sorry."

She pulled the door closed and locked it again.

"I just want to see her," Reese said. She looked like she was close to tears.

My father had told us there had been an outbreak

in a couple of nursing homes, but I couldn't say that to Reese. I didn't want her getting even more upset.

"Old people are the ones most at risk, so it's a good thing they're doing this. It's to protect her. That's good, right?" I said.

"I guess. I wish I could say hello."

"Which unit is hers?" Isaac asked.

"Two fourteen. Around the back."

"And all of them have balconies, right?"

"Yes..."

"Call her and tell her to go out on the balcony," Isaac said.

Reese took out her phone and punched in the numbers as we walked to the back of the building.

"Hello, Gran, it's me—it's Reese! Could you go out on your balcony?" I couldn't hear her answer. "It's a surprise. Just go. Okay...okay, bye."

We got to the back in time to see her grandmother appear at the railing of her balcony. We stopped right underneath her.

"Gran, it's me!" she yelled.

"Reese! Why don't you come up? I have cookies for you!"

"They won't let us in!" Reese said.

"Just go in the door. It's around the other side. Just come in."

"Reese, I don't think she understands," I said quietly.

Reese nodded. "You're right." She looked up at her grandmother. "Gran, my friends and I were just passing by and wanted to say hello."

Isaac started waving and yelled, "Hello!" and I did the same.

"We have to go, Gran," Reese said. "I love you. See you soon."

"I love you, my angel. Goodbye! Love you."

She disappeared from view, and we heard the sliding door above us close.

"That was hard, really hard," said Reese.

"But you saw her, and she saw you. I'm sure this whole thing won't last long, and soon you'll be able to visit her again," I said.

I hoped what I'd said was comforting to Reese. But I wasn't sure I believed it.

Chapter Six

My mom was doing much of the cooking now, since she was home most of the time. Sometimes I made dinner, but usually I just helped out. We always made up a serving for my father. We put his meal on a paper plate—with a second one covering it—and left it on the landing of the stairs. He used the microwave in the basement to heat it up.

"This looks, um, creative," I said as I looked at the dish on the table.

"It's my version of Mexican chicken delight. But I think I made it a little bit too spicy."

"I'm just going to grab some water for us." I got up and went to the fridge. I brought back a big pitcher and filled our glasses. "Did you do anything interesting today?"

"If you consider six hours of conference calls interesting, then I'm having a great time," said Mom. "What about you? Did you do anything fun?"

"I went for a bike ride with Reese and Isaac to see Reese's grandmother."

"The one in the home?" my mother said.

"Yeah, but they wouldn't let us in."

"That's not surprising. Your dad told me there's going to be an announcement tomorrow morning about all long-term care residences going on lock-down. Guess they got a jump on it. The virus is especially dangerous for the elderly, and staff have to do everything they can to keep them safe."

"Right," I said. I tried not to think about Reese's gran and how awful it would be if she got sick.

"The government is also going to require all nonessential services and businesses to close down temporarily," Mom continued.

"Nonessential?" I repeated.

"Grocery stores, gas stations and pharmacies, as well as hospitals, obviously, are considered essential services. They will remain open. Everything else, like clothing stores, malls, barbershops, hair salons and gyms, will be closed as of the end of business day tomorrow."

"Wow," I said. "I didn't think things would get this bad."

"Yes. And now we all have to do what we can to 'flatten the curve'—to slow down the spread."

"This is really serious, isn't it?" I asked.

"Yes, honey, it really is."

I expected her to say more, but she didn't.

"How many people have died?"

"There have been deaths around the world."

"But here at dad's hospital?"

"More than he expected. The steps I just mentioned are being taken to try to get in front of it. They're doing all the right things." She paused. "And there's one other thing you should know about that will be announced tomorrow, Quinn. They're going to delay the opening of schools for another two weeks."

"Two more weeks!" I had been happy about the longer spring break at first. But I really missed my friends. I even missed being in class and doing assignments.

"Yes, but the email I got from your principal explained that your teachers have been working hard at setting up a system so that you can do your classes from home."

So *that's* what Reese was talking about. I was actually looking forward to hearing more about it. And it would be nice to be in class with my friends again, even if it was only on my computer.

"Let's leave the rest of this talk for later," said Mom. "Dig in! And tell me, do you think your dad will like my surprise Mexican chicken delight?"

Chapter Seven

I walked out of the house and took a deep breath. Deep breaths were good. They calmed me down. We'd started online classes this week, and I'd just finished a lesson with Miss Fernandez. I didn't know why I found the Zoom sessions so stressful. Was it that I was staring at everybody? No, it was that I felt like they were all staring at me.

My father had left before I'd gotten up. I'd heard him go. My bedroom was right above the garage, and I could always hear the motor of the automatic opener purring and then the door itself grinding and groaning as it opened or closed.

My mother was upstairs in her new office, working away. She was wearing earbuds, so she couldn't really hear me, but she was speaking so loudly I could hear her throughout the entire house. I'd seen her briefly at breakfast, but that was about it before she'd headed upstairs to start work.

I looked around. Our street had never been what you'd call busy, but today there was absolutely nothing happening. Nobody out walking their dog, nobody on their bike, no cars. It was like an episode of *The Walking Dead*, minus the zombies.

"How's it going?"

I jumped up into the air and almost out of my skin. Isaac.

"I didn't mean to scare you," he said. He was sitting in a lawn chair right in front of his garage.

"What are you doing out here?"

"Probably the same as you," he said. "Taking a break. How's everybody doing at your place?"

"My mother's working from home, but I hardly ever see her, and my father is working so much he's hardly ever home."

"Same here," Isaac said. "My mom working so much, I mean."

"I thought the police wouldn't be so busy with everybody staying home."

"There's been a few break-ins at stores that are closed. And it's not always easy getting people to follow the new rules about not gathering in parks and public places."

"How did you like today's lesson?"

"I hate Zoom."

"You hate that Miss Fernandez figured out how to mute everybody's microphone," I said.

"I don't like that she learned how to mute *my* microphone."

"I think she might want to figure out how to keep doing that when we go back to our regular classroom." I was giving him a hard time, but the truth was, I missed his fooling around in class. He always made me laugh.

"Don't give her ideas. I just want to go back to school."

"You? The guy who cheered for the longer break?"

"Yeah, but it's been so long that I'm missing school. Well, at least, I'm missing playing sports and hanging with my friends and joking around and having lunch together and—"

"So nothing to do with actual learning."

"School has almost nothing to do with school," Isaac declared.

We saw someone come around the corner on a bike. As the person got closer, I realized it was better than "someone"—it was Reese! Isaac got out of his chair, and we both walked down our separate driveways toward the road. Reese stopped in front of my house—a safe six feet away. It was amazing how quickly we'd gotten used to the new rules.

"Hey, Reese," I said.

"Hey. It's so nice to be outside! I like the quiet. Do you know what it's like to have both parents at home trying to work?"

"Twice as bad as having one?" I offered.

"It feels like one of those exponential things, way more than double. All the teachers are trying to figure out this online-education stuff as they go. And they also have to deal with parents telling them they're doing it all wrong," Reese said.

"Miss Fernandez is doing a pretty good job," I said. "I don't love the screen part, but she is making the class interesting."

"I hate Zoom," Isaac said.

"You hate that Miss Fernandez has figured out the mute button," Reese countered.

Both Isaac and I started laughing. "Quinny just said the same thing. Am I that predictable?"

"These days you're about the only thing that is predictable," I said.

"Speaking of that," he said. "Time to update."

He pulled a piece of bright blue sidewalk chalk out of his pocket and walked onto the street. We watched as he added a stroke to mark the eleventh day.

"Has it really only been that long?" I asked.

"What do you mean?"

"It feels like it's been forever."

We all stood there—spread out—staring at the tally marks. The chalk on the driveway made it all seem more real.

"Is it just me or did you two find the assignment to explain flattening the curve totally confusing?" Isaac asked.

"No, I get it," I said. "My mom was telling me about it last week."

"I was a bit confused," Reese admitted.

"Well, Quinny, maybe you could explain it

to me," Isaac said. "You did a great job last time. Remember? Back in the olden days, when we had a classroom?"

"I can try," I said. "Go grab that cake pan your mom uses to make cinnamon buns, and a pitcher full of water and, um, an action figure of some kind."

"You're screwing with me, right?"

"Only one way to find out. Besides, are you doing anything else right now?"

"Point taken." He ran into the house.

"It's really good to see you," Reese said.

"We were just on Zoom together!" I replied, surprised.

"Yeah, but it's different in person. It's nice to spend time face-to-face."

"You're right. It's good to see you too. How's your grandmother doing?"

"She's okay, but they told us there are two staff and five residents who have contracted the virus now. They're in isolation. We talk to Gran on the phone every day, but I wish we could see her."

"I hope this doesn't go on much longer."

"Does anybody really know though?" Reese asked.

"That's the worst part. How many more tally marks does Isaac have to add before it's over?"

"Your father would know better than anybody, wouldn't he?"

"Well, he's saying nobody knows for sure, but he's still certain we're doing the right things."

Isaac reappeared, carrying a plastic jug and the metal pan. He was going so fast that some of the water sloshed out of the pitcher and onto his pants. "Oh, great. Now it looks like I peed myself!" he cried. "Where do you want this stuff?"

"Put them both down on the driveway." Reese and I watched him do that. "Now pour all the water from the pitcher into the cake pan."

"There's too much in here—it'll overflow."

"Just do it."

Isaac picked up the pitcher and started to pour. He kept going until the pitcher was empty and the pan was full almost to the top.

"Wow. I didn't think all that water would fit in there," he said.

"It's the same amount of water in both, but it's spread out in the pan. That's what it means to flatten the curve."

"And why is that important?" he asked.

"Did you bring the action figure?"

He pulled a small plastic Spider-Man out of his pocket.

"Make him stand up in the pan."

"Again, are you just screwing with me?"

I smirked. He put the figure in the pan.

"See how the water is only up to his knees? What would happen if he was standing at the bottom of the pitcher? With the same amount of water in it?"

"Assuming he couldn't swim, he'd be underwater, in big trouble," Isaac said. "So what you're saying is that we're trying to flatten the curve so we don't drown Spider-Man."

"Or anybody, especially old people. And we have to make sure our hospitals don't get too crowded, so doctors and nurses can take care of those who are infected."

"I get it now. But boy, would you have looked stupid if I'd brought out Aquaman!"

"Ha ha. You're the one who looks like he peed himself, and *I'm* the one who would look stupid?"

"I better get going," Reese said. "Guess I'll see you on Zoom."

I wished I could give her a hug. I watched her ride off.

I turned to Isaac. "Hey, so I'm going in to make lunch for me and Mom. Do you want to join us?"

"You're not inviting me in, are you?"

"Not inside. But Mom and I could eat in our backyard and you could eat in yours. Like a strange kind of picnic," I said.

"Normally I'd tell you how lame that is."

"And now?"

"This ain't normal. See you in twenty minutes."

Chapter Eight

"Good evening, Mrs. Singh, your dog is looking particularly nice today," Isaac called out.

Mrs. Singh and her dog were walking by our houses. Isaac and I were sitting on our separate chairs on our separate driveways. Watching the world go by.

"Thank you, Isaac. I was the one who gave him his new haircut."

"You did a great job," I added. "Do you think you can loan Isaac's mother your shears so she can do his hair?"

Mrs. Singh laughed. "He *is* looking a little bit shaggy. But aren't we all?" She put her hands up to her center part. "Look at how my roots are showing!"

"I think that stripe looks cool," said Isaac. "Have a great walk."

"Say hello to your parents for me. Good evening."

Mrs. Singh was part of the regular parade that walked past our house each night. After dinner lots of people went out for a stroll—little family groups—or sat on their porches or in their driveways, talking to the people passing by. Everyone seemed extra friendly. Isaac and I met every night on our driveways at seven fifteen. We sat out for as long as we felt like. Sometimes it was until after dark.

Isaac had taken his chalk and decorated the entire sidewalk and road in front of his house. He'd marked out hopscotch courts, drawn flowers and even written jokes. Most of them were bad, sort of an Isaac version of dad jokes, but people often stopped, looked and laughed. They must have been *really* bored.

After Mrs. Singh, a couple and their two kids passed by. The woman was carrying the baby in a carrier, and the little girl was riding circles around her parents on a small bike with training wheels. When they got to the part of the road in front of Isaac's house, the girl got off her bike and grabbed her dad's hand. She made him hop along the hopscotch court with her. By the end they were both laughing, and I couldn't help but smile. Finished, the girl got back on her bike.

"You are *sooo* good on your bike," Isaac called out. The little girl beamed.

"Thank you for doing all of this," the father said. "This is one of Claire's highlights every night."

"You're welcome," Isaac said. "And your family passing by is one of my highlights."

The whole family waved goodbye and continued on their way.

"I don't know how you do it," I said.

"Do what?"

"You just seem so positive all the time."

Isaac shrugged. "Maybe it's because I'm not smart enough to be as worried as I should be. Now you, Quinny, are a different thing."

"I'm not—"

"Stop it. Do I have remind you how well I know you? I know you get scared and anxious about things, but I also know you don't let that stop you from doing what needs to be done. So on a scale of one to ten, how worried are you?"

I shrugged. "I don't know...a seven? Mostly about my father."

"You should be. Wait, that sounded wrong. What I mean is, I understand why you're worried. Your dad is on the front lines. It's only natural that you'd be worried. How bad are things getting?"

"I don't see him much. Our conversations are either on the phone or with me on the landing and him at the bottom of the stairs."

"I heard the cases are going up day by day. Really going up."

"I've been watching the news, and I know the numbers are increasing, but I can't watch too much of it...well, I just can't."

The numbers *were* going up—of new cases, of people going to hospital and, worse, of people dying. Every day there were more.

"But they're just *numbers*. Your father sees *people*. That makes it different. I've heard about shortages. Are they running out of equipment and PPE at the hospital?" Isaac asked.

"No. I don't think so. Who did you hear that from?"

"You're not the only one who watches the news. Has your father mentioned anything about that?"

"No, he hasn't." Not that he would. I didn't want to talk about this anymore.

Isaac must have picked up on that. He got up from his chair. "Do you want to go for a walk? Keeping our distance, of course."

"Where to?"

"Just around. I need to move my legs."

"Okay, let's go."

I walked on the sidewalk and Isaac stayed on the road, a few feet away from me. When we came to other people, we nodded or said hello and then moved far enough aside to let them pass.

We went for a ways along the same path we had taken to see Reese's grandmother, then turned toward our local shopping strip. That's where the grocery store was, along with McCormick's Bakery and the ice-cream shop we went to after soccer games.

"I'd kill for a rocky road triple scoop right now," Isaac said. "How can ice cream not be considered an essential service?"

"You know, everything seems so normal. Well, except for the lineup." I motioned to the people queued up outside the grocery store.

"See how they're spaced out?" Isaac asked. "That's the way they're supposed to be doing it. My mother says that sometimes people aren't doing the right things. The police got called for the toilet-paper wars."

"I heard about that on the news, but I didn't know it had happened here."

"Three squad cars. It was so crazy they almost had to make arrests because people were fighting over toilet paper. My mother said it only proved what she's always believed, that some people are full of crap."

We made a turn into the park and passed the empty playground. Swings were now tied together with cords so they wouldn't work, and yellow caution tape surrounded the whole thing. Farther along were the tennis and basketball courts. The nets and rims had been removed. Beyond that were the soccer fields. Where once there would have been multiple games going on, there was only a father and daughter, kicking a ball back and forth.

"Do you think it'll ever go back to the way it was?" I asked.

"It changed so fast. I can't see why it can't change back fast too."

"I heard we have to wait until they find a vaccine."

"I'm sure there are lots of smart people working on it," Isaac said. "Sometimes you just have to have faith."

Chapter Nine

I heard the garage door open and put down my books. Schoolwork could wait. My mother was home. I ran down the hall and opened the door that led into the garage. My mom had parked on the driveway and was climbing out of her car.

"Hey, Mom, how was shopping?"

"I never thought buying groceries could be so exciting and scary at the same time." She popped open the trunk and grabbed some bags.

"Here, let me help," I said as I ran toward her.

"No!" she practically shouted. I skidded to a surprised stop. "Sorry—I mean, no, I don't want you to touch them. But if you want, you can sit on the steps and keep me company."

I backed away and sat down. I watched as Mom started removing bags and placing them on the floor of the garage.

"Was it crowded?"

"There was a lineup outside. It looked longer than it was because everybody was standing six feet apart. Once I got in, it wasn't that bad. Just so different."

I hadn't been able to go shopping with her because only one person from a family was allowed to go into the store.

"Between the one-way arrows for the aisles, people staying apart, plexiglass shields at the cash registers and, of course, gloves and masks, it's all so surreal." She gestured to the white mask still hanging around her neck.

"You sure bought a lot of stuff, Mom."

"Yes, it's amazing how much you need to last two weeks," she said as she kept pulling out bags. "It's not more than we'd normally buy, but it's all at once. I made sure to get only what we need so there'd be plenty left for other people."

"Dad says that's how everybody should be doing it."

"He's right."

"Is he coming home tonight?" I asked.

"I'm not sure, honey. He never knows how his day is going to go until it's done."

Once all the bags were out of the car, my mother started taking items from them and spreading them out on the floor in little groups—meat, milk, fruit and vegetables, cans, cartons and boxes, and frozen items.

"I've always thought the hardest part of shopping was putting stuff away when you got home. Now it's even harder," she said.

She started moving items to a big blue Tupperware container. These were things that didn't need to be refrigerated and could be stored for a few days. That way any virus on those items would die just by sitting there.

Next she started to bring fruit and vegetables over to the counter by the laundry sink.

"How was school today?" she asked.

"Same as always. It's not too bad, but I'm really tired of all this."

She ran hot water and put in some soap. As the sink filled up, she continued to bring over more items.

"I think we're all tired of everything, but it's just the way it is right now."

"I know. But I miss my friends."

"I know it's hard, honey. We're missing so much. But what I miss more than anything is your father being here with us. He's working so hard to keep all of us safe. We need to be grateful for the people who are missing seeing their families in order to keep everyone safe."

I felt selfish for being so upset about not seeing my friends. I missed my dad so much. But I hadn't really thought about how much he missed *us*.

Mom started dipping fruits and vegetables in the sink and scrubbing them with a little brush. She rinsed off each item with fresh water and placed it on the counter until she was finished. Next she started bringing over milk cartons and containers of yogurt and packaged salads. She wiped them all down with the soapy solution.

"Do you think everything you're doing is necessary?" I asked.

"It can't hurt, right?" She looked at me. Maybe she could see I was feeling anxious, because she asked, "How are you doing, Quinn?"

"Fine."

"Really?"

I let out a big breath. "I get nervous sometimes, but who doesn't? I think I'm doing okay, don't you?"

"I think you're doing amazing. It can be pretty overwhelming."

Overwhelming was the perfect word. That was how I felt sometimes. I had trouble getting to sleep because I couldn't stop thinking about it. When was it ever going to end? Right there in the garage, I felt my lower lip start to quiver. My mother didn't need to see that. She had enough to worry about. I was glad her attention was on the groceries and not on me.

"Tell me more about how the online learning is going."

"Not sure if there's much to tell. Some of the assignments are okay, and others, well, they're as useless as always."

"It must be difficult for your teachers," she said.

"I know the teachers are trying. It's just hard for us to focus on math or science when there's so much happening out there in the real world."

"What kind of assignment would you like to do instead?"

"Well, we had one about what it meant to flatten the curve and I really liked that. So, for example, what if when we do stats, it was about COVID-19? Couldn't we be studying the virus in science? What about writing in our journals about how this feels to us?"

"Wouldn't it make it harder if more of your school assignments were about the virus?" my mother asked. "Don't you want to get away from it sometimes?"

"There is no getting away from it! I think having more information, talking about it, will make it better. I get anxious about things I don't understand."

"Well, maybe you can suggest some of those ideas to Miss Fernandez. She's good about things like that, isn't she?"

"I guess so."

"I'm glad you're spending time with Isaac," she said. "It must be hard for him being alone so much."

"We keep each other company. Besides, he doesn't do well without an audience."

"It was nice that he joined us for lunch the other day."

"Yeah," I said, getting up. I had had enough of this serious talk. "I better get going on my schoolwork."

"Thanks for offering to help with the groceries," my mom said. "Sorry if I barked at you."

"That's okay. I understand."

"I'm just trying to keep you safe. But it was nice talking to you. I think you should talk to Miss Fernandez about doing something more *real* as an assignment."

"I'll think about it. And…Mom?"

"Yes?"

"Thanks for everything."

Chapter Ten

I settled onto the landing of the stairs. I balanced my plate on my lap. My father took a seat at the bottom, twelve steps away. Even from here I could see how marked his face was from the mask. And his hands were raw. He was washing and sanitizing his hands so often that the alcohol was irritating the skin.

"How's my Q-Cat? It's nice to have you join me for dinner."

"It *is* nice." We weren't sitting together, but it still felt good.

"I was hoping your mother would join us. I'm surprised she's still working."

"I'm surprised you're not," I replied without

thinking. I'd only meant that he wasn't usually home for dinner.

"I'm sorry. It must be tough for you to have both of us being so busy. So many people aren't working right now, and the two of us seem to be working harder than ever."

"I shouldn't have said anything. I know what you're doing is important. And hard."

"Does it show that much?" He rubbed his hands against the creases in his face.

"I didn't just mean the marks."

We sat and ate in silence for a while. Was he trying to figure out what to say or was he just too tired to say anything?

"You know, this time here with you," he said, "helps remind me why I'm doing this."

I wondered if I should bother him with the things I'd been worried about. I decided I had to ask. "Dad?"

"What is it, Q-Cat?"

"I've been seeing things on the news and…well, I just wondered if the hospital has enough PPE for everyone."

"We're taking every precaution to keep us safe.

We have enough at the hospital for now. The real concern is in places like nursing homes."

"Like where Reese's grandmother lives?"

"All long-term care facilities. They're scrambling to provide equipment for their staff."

"But that's not fair. Everything I've seen on the news and the internet says that old people are the most at risk."

"It sounds like you're spending a lot of time on the internet," he said.

"I am, but what else is there to do?"

"Be careful. There's a lot of misinformation out there."

"Am I wrong about the old people?"

"No. Older people and those with pre-existing medical problems, like heart conditions, diabetes or breathing difficulties, are at higher risk. A high percentage of the deaths have been people over seventy."

Deaths. That was something he hardly ever mentioned.

"Have there been a lot of deaths at the hospital?"

"More than I've ever seen." His words were quiet, his voice so serious. "It's important that we keep doing what we're doing to flatten that curve of new infections."

"Is it working?"

"It's not flat yet, but it's flattening. We just have to keep doing the right things. Some people think this is the time to relax, but it's not. If you're racing downhill and you're trying to slow down enough that you don't crash, you don't take your foot off the brake. We need to press down harder."

"That makes sense." There was something else I wanted to ask him, but I wasn't sure how to ask it. Maybe I'd go around it a bit. "Are people scared at the hospital?"

"Patients or staff?"

"Both, I guess."

"Patients are scared because of what they *don't* know. Staff are scared because of what they *do* know."

"Are *you* scared, Dad?" That was what I really wanted to know.

"I'd be lying if I said I wasn't."

"Don't you sometimes feel like you just don't want to go to work?"

"Some days. But I don't have a choice. No more

than those people working at the grocery store, or the aides at the nursing homes, or police officers, paramedics—there are so many of us. These are our jobs. Do you still think you might want to be a doctor when you grow up?"

"More than ever."

"If you were a doctor, would you stop doing your job?"

"No—at least, I don't think I would. I hope I wouldn't be too scared," I said.

"If being scared stopped us, then almost nobody would be there. Maybe the fear makes us work even safer."

My mother suddenly appeared at the top of the stairs. "Is it too late to join you two?"

"We're pretty well finished, but having you join us is the best dessert I can imagine," my father said.

"I have to disagree. Did you know that McCormick's Bakery started home delivery?"

"You don't mean...?" I think my dad's grin was bigger than mine.

"I had a pineapple upside down cake dropped off at the door. Surprise! I'm going to go get a piece for everybody."

Chapter Eleven

Miss Fernandez was talking, and I was trying hard to stay focused. Her face was in a square in the center of the screen, and there were eighteen other little squares around it—our entire class.

As she talked, I stared at her. She was dressed in a gray sweatshirt. It had a little stain by the collar. She wasn't wearing any makeup, and her hair was messy. Behind her I could see a picture on the wall, a bookcase and a cluttered table. Sometimes her cat jumped up onto her desk and joined the class. He hadn't appeared yet today, and I missed him.

My square on the screen was in the middle and toward the bottom. I was grateful that it wasn't big enough for others to see more than my face and a little bit of my clothing. I was still wearing my pajama bottoms. I wondered if Miss Fernandez was too.

I looked from square to square, locating my friends and classmates. Reese was on the left. She'd asked a few questions. Isaac was close to the top. He would be there for a while, gone briefly and then reappear. I pictured him wandering around his house the way he normally wandered around the class.

"I will be emailing the assignment," Miss Fernandez said. "You have until Friday afternoon to send in the completed work. Are there any questions?"

A number of people electronically "raised" their hands. I did too. She started addressing them person by person, unmuting each microphone so we could all hear the question. Some students asked things they should have known if they'd been listening. Some things didn't change whether we were in class or in a Zoom session.

"Hello, Quinn. You have a question?" Miss Fernandez asked.

I had spaced out, so I was thrown, and I hesitated before starting. "Uh…it isn't about this assignment.

It's about something new."

"Please, go ahead."

"I thought it would be nice if we could do something a bit more practical."

"Go on."

"I heard there's a shortage of personal protective equipment. Masks."

"I've heard that as well. What do you have in mind?"

"I thought that maybe we could make some masks."

"I'm afraid that many of us don't have a sewing machine or any skills."

"You don't need either of those. There are videos online about how to sew masks by hand. I even made one to try it out."

I pulled it up and held it in front of the camera. Miss Fernandez did something with the controls, and suddenly my face and the mask were in the big square in the middle. Now I wished I had washed my hair.

"Wow, Quinn. I am very impressed."

"There are patterns you can download, and it's explained really well."

"And what would we do with these masks?" Miss Fernandez asked.

"We could donate them to the staff at Vista Village Lodge. Reese's grandmother lives there."

"That makes it even more special. Reese, would you like that?" Miss Fernandez asked.

I knew Reese was on board because we'd already talked about it.

"I'd like that a lot," Reese replied.

"All in favor of this project, please raise your hands," Miss Fernandez said.

I saw a whole bunch of little electronic hands go up.

"Then it's unanimous. We'll work out the details. Now are there any more questions before we break for the day?…Yes, Isaac?"

I looked down at his square. What the heck was he wearing? Miss Fernandez began to laugh, and a new center square came on. It was somebody—it had to be Isaac—wearing a hockey goalie's mask.

"I was wondering, would this work?" he asked.

Miss Fernandez was laughing louder, and I could see other people giggling and pointing.

"And if that didn't work, how about this?" Isaac asked. He pulled off the goalie mask and replaced it with a Spider-Man mask.

I was laughing now, and I could hear other people chuckling as well. Miss Fernandez must have unmuted everybody's microphones. It felt so good to hear their laughter, to share their joy. And for those few seconds it felt like we weren't alone in our little electronic video squares and houses and apartments.

"Isaac, I have truly missed you," Miss Fernandez said. "I've missed everyone. Thank you all for joining us today."

Chapter Twelve

Reese and I sat on our bikes and waited as Isaac finished his chalk tally sheet. It had rained the night before—it had been raining a lot the last week. He traced over each of the strokes and then added today's mark. It was day 36.

"Did you ever think it would last so long?" Reese asked.

"I don't think anybody did. Who could have imagined any of this?"

Isaac looked up from his work. "Seven weeks ago, if you were wearing masks, sanitizing your hands fifteen times a day and washing your groceries when you came home, people would have thought it more than a little strange."

"Now if you *weren't* doing all those things it would be strange," I said.

Isaac climbed on his bike, and we started off. "There are still some people who think this whole thing is ridiculous. My mother told me there's going to be a protest in the park."

"What are they protesting?" Reese asked.

"They think the virus is fake."

"*Fake?* People are *dying*. How is that fake?" I asked.

"Some of them are business owners who want to reopen because they're losing money. And others say they'd rather be dead than give up their freedom."

"Lucky them. They might get their wish," I said.

"They might also get a fine. Protesters who get too close to each other are going to get an $800 ticket for not practicing physical distancing."

"Turn up ahead," I said.

"Yes, ma'am."

We came to our first stop. Jenna was sitting on her front lawn. She got up as we approached and waved hello. We yelled out greetings as we came to a stop, making sure we weren't too close to her or each other. She looked pretty happy to see us. She held up a little plastic bag.

"How many?" Isaac asked.

"Seven."

"Way to go, Jenna! Just leave the bag on the edge of the sidewalk," Reese said.

She put it down and backed away. Reese was wearing clear latex gloves. She picked up the bag and put it into a big blue plastic box strapped to the back of her bike. This was the first stop of many. What had started with just our class had grown to include almost every student from every class in our whole grade.

"Do you three remember the last time we were all together?" I asked.

Nobody answered. I had to remind them. "We were planning the spring dance."

"Hard to believe that was our biggest worry," Jenna said. "Well, Isaac wasn't that worried even then."

"Like I said, it's a dance. I could plan something like that in my sleep. Anyway, we have to get going," Isaac said. "One stop down and another gazillion to go."

- 😊 -

"Raise your hand if you're tired," Reese said.

"I think I'm too tired to raise a hand," Isaac replied.

"It was fun to see everybody," I answered.

The best part about collecting masks had been visiting people in real life instead of in a Zoom session or on Facetime. I couldn't believe how much I'd missed them all. Everybody had been excited to see us, and a bunch had even started crying. I'd almost starting crying a few times myself.

Now we were making our final stop. Vista Village Lodge. We could see that there were lots of people out on their balconies. They started to clap and cheer and whistle. A big handmade sign, painted in red on a white bedsheet, was draped over the front door. It read, *Thank you, Switzerland Point Middle School Students!*

We stopped and got off our bikes.

"Definitely worth the ride," Isaac said. He pulled out his camera. "You two keep going. I want to get this on video."

Reese unstrapped the plastic bin from her bike, and we walked toward the door. The cheers got louder. The door opened, and a woman in a nurse's uniform, wearing a mask, came out. But there was another person with her. It was Reese's grandmother! She was also wearing a mask.

Reese and I stopped with a safe distance between us. I knew that both of us weren't far from tears. Reese put down the bin. "Here are the masks we made. So many students contributed."

"We can't thank you enough," said the nurse. "This is so very kind of you."

"It was the least we could do," I said. "Thank you for all you're doing to keep everyone safe."

"Reese, darling, it's so good to see you," said her grandmother.

"You too, Gran. I just wish I could hug you, but you know I can't."

"You already gave everyone here the best hug you could," the nurse said. "You kids are wonderful."

The nurse started crying. And so did Reese. And so did I.

Chapter Thirteen

"It's coming on again!" my mother yelled. She turned the sound up on the TV.

"*Sometimes the worst of times brings out the best in people,*" the announcer said.

The picture changed. It was the video shot by Isaac. He'd shared the footage in a Zoom session with our class and then put it up online. At first it was just kids from our grade and their parents viewing it, then the whole school. And then it was picked up by a local TV station. It jumped from 450 views to over 20,000 in two days. Now they kept showing it on the news.

"And that's Quinny and Reese's Pieces." Isaac's voice could be heard as we walked toward the door. "The names sound like a couple of chocolate bars. Which makes sense, since they are two of the sweetest girls you'll ever meet."

I'd heard it a dozen times, but I still smiled. Thank goodness he'd gone with Quinny instead of Q-Ball or Q-Tip or one of the other half dozen names he had for me.

"Quinny had the idea to make the masks, and that older woman who just came out with the nurse, that's Reese's grandmother," Isaac could be heard saying.

The screen showed us walking to a spot a safe distance from the entrance and Reese putting down the blue bin.

"Our whole class made masks to give to the staff and residents of Vista Village. Big shout-out to Miss Fernandez, our wonderful teacher, all the eighth-grade students of Switzerland Point Middle School—go, Panthers, go—and our principal, Mrs. Reynolds."

"And now you see that the nurse is crying...and Reese is crying...and Quinny is crying."

Isaac's voice cracked over the last few words.

"I'm not crying—*you're* crying," Isaac said, even though it was obvious who was really crying.

The scene shifted back to the anchorwoman. Behind her was a picture of Reese, Isaac and me.

"*I've seen this story half a dozen times, and it still makes me tear up,*" the anchorwoman said. "*And to add some background to the story, the young man who shot the footage on his phone and narrated is Isaac Peters. His mother is the police chief in Dansville. Reese Ellis's parents are teachers at the local elementary and high schools. And the young girl behind the idea, Quinn Arseneau, her father is an emergency room doctor working the front lines. This makes it an even more heartwarming story — our entire community is pulling together to support one another. Please remember that even when we stand apart, we still stand together.*"

My mother turned off the TV. She sniffed a bit and wiped away a couple of tears.

"I am so proud of you, Quinn." She gave me a big hug, and I hugged her back.

"Now I better get to work. And don't you have a Zoom session coming up?"

"In a few minutes."

My mother went to her office, and I went to the kitchen and opened my computer. I clicked on the link. Some people had already joined the session. Miss Fernandez welcomed me in. She did that with everyone as they joined. She said it was her way of "greeting us at the door." It felt nice.

I looked from square to square. I missed these people. It wasn't like we hadn't been in contact, because I'd touched base with almost everybody on the screen almost every day. I'd talked to my best friends, of course, but also to people I'd never really talked with much before. I had found out things about them I hadn't known. We were an interesting, quirky and unusual group, and I was really looking forward to the time we could be together again.

Miss Fernandez called the class to order by muting all the microphones.

"Our efforts to help our community by making masks have certainly been well received," she began.

We could see one another clapping and cheering, even if we couldn't hear it.

"This is important to remember. Even though we're isolated, we can still come together. So, well done, everyone." She looked down at some papers in front of her. "I have an announcement to read to you. It's being shared across our board and with the media later today."

Uh-oh. This was either going to be really good or really bad. I felt nervous.

Miss Fernandez looked up from the papers. "Look, I'm not going to read the official release. I'm going to tell you what's going on, and then you can ask questions." She paused for a moment and then began to speak again. "Last night the trustees of the board of education held a virtual meeting. They decided that schools in the district will remain closed for the rest of the school year."

I felt like I'd been kicked in the stomach.

Miss Fernandez kept talking. I didn't hear much. I was watching the reactions of my classmates. Some had their hands covering their faces, others looked like they were crying, and some had just walked away. I went from square to square, looking for Isaac. I knew he'd been in the session, but now I couldn't find him. I didn't want to be here either. I left my computer. I needed to tell my mother.

When I got to the bottom of the stairs, I could hear her talking. She was in the middle of a meeting, and from what I could tell, it wasn't going well. I couldn't interrupt.

I turned and went through the door to the garage. I hit the button to raise the big doors. The door creaked as it opened. I passed by the table full of quarantined groceries and thought for a second about getting on my bike and just going for a ride. Then I heard the pinging of a basketball.

Isaac was on his driveway. He stopped bouncing the ball when he saw me.

"Are you okay?" he asked.

I shrugged. "You?"

"When Miss Fernandez started talking, I really thought she was going to tell us we'd be going back to school. Maybe not right away, but in a few weeks or even a month. I didn't expect it to be over."

"We will still have our lessons and Zoom and—"

"And no getting together or lunches in the cafeteria or pickup games at recess or team sports or the end-of-the-year class trip or graduation or the dance."

"I never thought the dance would be one of the things you'd miss."

"Maybe not the way Jenna is going to miss it, but it's one of the things we won't get to do. Wait— did Miss Fernandez end the session?"

"No, I just didn't want to hear any more."

"I never thought I'd see the day when Quinny Arseneau walked out of class, even a virtual class. You should go back."

"So should you," I said.

"I'm going for a walk."

"Do you want company? I mean, you know, physically distant company?"

He shook his head. "I think I need to be alone. I have some things to think about."

Chapter Fourteen

I heard the sound of the garage door opening. My father was home. I reached over and grabbed my phone. It was 12:35 a.m. I'd thought he was just going to sleep at the hospital tonight. He was doing that at least twice a week. I couldn't imagine how tired he must be.

I plumped up my pillows and shifted around, trying to make myself more comfortable so I could get to sleep. For more than an hour I had been trying the usual things I did to slow down my thoughts, but nothing was working. Who was I fooling? There was no way I was going to sleep anytime soon.

I climbed out of bed. There was a night-light on in the hall. The door to my parents' bedroom was closed, and I couldn't hear the sound of the TV. My mother was asleep. She'd said she was so tired at the end of each day now that she slept like a log.

I tiptoed down the stairs. The light over the stove was dim but just bright enough for me to see. The door to the basement was shut, but there was a faint glow coming from under the door. I opened it. Lights were definitely on, but I didn't hear anything. My father couldn't already be asleep, could he? If he was, I didn't want to wake him.

Carefully, and as quietly as possible, I went down the stairs. When I reached the landing, I stopped. This was as far as I was allowed to go. It was silent… and then I heard a sound. It didn't register at first, but then I got it. It was the sound of somebody crying. My father was crying. Was he hurt?

"Dad!" I called out.

The sound stopped, and I heard footfalls, and then he appeared at the bottom of the stairs. He was still in his blue scrubs. "Q-Cat, are you all right?"

"I heard you come home."

"Sorry. I didn't mean to wake anybody up."

"You didn't wake me because I wasn't asleep. Dad, are you okay?"

"I'm good."

"I heard you."

He didn't answer right away. "I'm sorry. I didn't want that. It was a bad day at the hospital."

"But I thought it was getting better."

"It is—out there. We're still dealing with it. There were just so many cases, so many..." His whole body seemed to shudder. "I heard about your school being closed for the rest of the school year. Is that why you can't sleep?"

"It's just school."

"It's not *just* school. It's your life. It's okay to be upset. But tomorrow the sun will rise, and eventually it's all going to be better."

"Do you really think so?"

"The sun is guaranteed to come up." He shrugged. "Every day we get a little closer. How about we plan on having supper tomorrow together, as a family?"

"We can do that?"

"We can sit in the backyard. You and your mom can be at the picnic bench, and I'll sit on a chair off to the side."

"Could Isaac join us from his yard?"

"Sure! Invite his mother too, if she's home. I'm learning that we can't do things the way we might want to, but we can still figure out ways to do the things that are important."

"That sounds great, Dad."

"Now, my girl, it's time for you to go upstairs and get some sleep. I'll try to do the same. See you tomorrow at dinner."

"Okay. Goodnight, Dad."

"Goodnight, Q-Cat."

Chapter Fifteen

"I want to thank you all for coming," I said.

I was sitting in my chair on my driveway. Isaac was on his. Reese and Jenna were leaning against their bikes on the road in front of our houses.

"It's not like there was much else to do," Isaac said. "I've seen everything on Netflix."

"We've all been watching Netflix," Reese said.

"No, you don't understand. I've seen *everything* on Netflix. I started with the usual stuff, but eventually I found myself watching *Downton Abbey* and *The Crown*. I think I might have a crush on the queen—at least, the young queen."

Even now, Isaac was Isaac.

"If it helps, I could try to speak in an English

accent," I suggested.

"Pip! Pip! Just get on with it," he replied. "Why are we here?"

"I wanted to talk to you about the spring dance," I said.

"What's there to talk about?" Isaac asked.

"I want to discuss planning it," I said.

"You really need to pay more attention, Quinny. There's this thing they call a *pandemic*, and school has been canceled," Isaac said.

"Would you like to keep talking, or would you like me to explain?"

"I think explaining would be good," Reese said.

"Yeah, I'd like to hear what Quinn is getting at," Jenna added.

"It is going to mean a lot of work for us," I warned.

"I can do work, and believe me, I have time," Isaac said. "Let's hear your plan."

"It's more the *start* of my plan," I said.

"Just tell us, Quinn!" said Reese.

In a quick burst I gave them my idea.

"What do you think?" I asked. Every one of them was smiling.

"I'm in," Reese said.

"This could work," said Jenna. "Where do we start?"

"We need to get Miss Fernandez on board."

"And it wouldn't hurt to consult my mom," Isaac said. "We probably need her support."

"What about your dad, Quinn?" Reese asked. "It couldn't hurt to have a doctor sign off on it."

"Okay, I'll talk to Dad tonight. Isaac, see what your mom says."

"And how about we set up a Zoom conference with Miss Fernandez for later today?" Jenna suggested.

"Good. We have a plan. Now let's see if we can have a dance."

- 😊 -

It had taken three days to put it all together, get our parents to agree and convince Miss Fernandez to support us. Then we'd had to present the whole plan to Mrs. Reynolds to take to the board. Now we were all waiting for Mrs. Reynolds to join the Zoom conversation and let us know if we had permission to proceed. My mother and I were staring at my screen in the kitchen. My father was joining us from the hospital, Isaac was at his house, his mother was at the police station, Jenna was with her parents, and Reese was with hers. Miss Fernandez was the moderator. She had all the microphones unmuted, and there were multiple conversations going on. It seemed to me the parents were enjoying talking to one another even more than we kids were.

Mrs. Reynolds finally joined the session. Everybody greeted her, and then Miss Fernandez muted all the microphones except for hers and the principal's.

"Mrs. Reynolds, we're glad you can be here today. We're all waiting for your news."

"As you know, I brought your plan to the board," Mrs. Reynolds said. "I shared all the very thoughtful details you kids had carefully laid out. I explained that you had the support of your class, your teachers and your parents. I also told them that I, as the principal, supported your plan."

This was going to happen! It was going to happen!

"So I am very sorry to inform you they turned down your request."

My mother groaned, and I felt my heart sink. Little electronic hands popped up from my father and from Isaac's mother.

"They said that since the school is closed, there could not be a board-sanctioned dance."

"I'm so sorry to hear that," Miss Fernandez said. "I'm disappointed, and I know the students must be even more disappointed."

"However," Mrs. Reynolds said, "that doesn't mean you can't go ahead with your plan."

"What does she mean?" my mother asked me.

I shrugged. But we were about to get our answer.

"You cannot have a *school* dance. But there's nothing stopping you from organizing a community event. I'm going to leave that to you to decide." She paused. "I wish you all well."

Chapter Sixteen

I stood on the road, and Isaac stood on his driveway. At my feet were the tally marks. There were 47 marks for 47 days.

"Looking pretty sharp, Quinny."

"Thank you."

I was in the red satin dress I had picked out ages ago. I had on low heels and a bit of makeup, and my mother had helped me with my hair.

"No comment about how good I look?" Isaac asked.

Isaac was in a shirt, tie and a jacket that was way too big. To complete his outfit, he wore bright red skateboarding shoes and matching red, baggy shorts. He had joked that this was "semi-formal done by Isaac."

"You look very handsome," I replied.

"I was going for stunning."

"Do you think anyone is even going to come?" I asked.

"What do you mean? There's already two of us. And Reese and Jenna will be here for sure."

"Well, because the school didn't agree to it, I'm not sure Jenna's parents are going to let her come."

"Okay, then three of us at least. Which means you can only expect every second dance with me. Don't be jealous." He paused. "I'm just kidding, Quinny. Don't worry. This is going to work."

I caught sight of flashing lights. Two police cars had pulled in so that together they blocked off the street at one end. I turned around in time to see more flashing lights. It was a third police car and an ambulance. They formed a barricade at the other end of the block.

"Why an ambulance?" I asked.

"Just the thing they do at parades and soccer games—you know, big public gatherings."

"So far not so big."

"There'll be more people," Isaac said. "Who would want to miss seeing all this?"

"It is pretty amazing."

Up and down the whole length of the block were boxes drawn on the street with chalk. Each box was ten feet by ten feet and was separated from the next one by six feet. There were two rows, with a six-foot strip between them. Each box was numbered, from 1 to 100. One hundred boxes for 100 guests, drawn so each person would remain at a safe distance from everybody else. It had taken us almost a full day to measure and mark them all off.

Isaac's mother came out of their house. She was in full uniform and carrying a police bullhorn.

"It's good to see my officers have arrived," she said. "You two look very nice."

"I think we've agreed that we're both stunning."

"Thank you for getting us permission to do this, Ms. Peters. And for agreeing to be one of the chaperones," I said.

"I think you kids need this. Maybe all of us do. Oh, look. Your first guests are arriving."

At the end of the street a couple of cars had pulled up. A kid got out of each. As the parents drove away, the kids were both let onto the street by the officers.

From this distance I couldn't tell who they were. The guy was in a suit, and the girl was in a formal, fancy, sparkly party dress—it was Jenna! The mask she was wearing had big red lips painted on it. Noah's mask had a big, burly mustache.

"Your parents let you come!" I exclaimed to Jenna as Isaac greeted Noah.

People had started to come out of their houses. They were setting up lawn chairs and sitting down on the edge of their properties. Every family on the street knew what we were doing. We had invited them to come out and listen and watch and cheer— their presence would just add to the atmosphere.

Cars kept pulling up at both ends of the street to drop off kids, and more and more of our classmates appeared. Some came by themselves, on bikes or on foot. As each person arrived, they went to their assigned spot. We had sent everybody an email telling them what they needed to know. They each knew their number and that they had to go to that square and stay apart from others. We had also made it clear that there would be no second chance for anybody who didn't respect physical distancing. Isaac's mom had insisted on that. Violating the rule meant being sent home. Each person had brought a backpack containing their supplies for the night—snacks, a water bottle or two, a set of earbuds and a phone.

A little cheer went up, and I turned to see Miss Fernandez arriving. She waved to people as she walked down the center strip and to her assigned square. Like everyone else, she was wearing a home-made mask. And her dress was fancy! She looked like she was ready to party, but she was also one of our chaperones, along with Isaac's mom and both of Reese's parents. It was good to have the police chief and teachers around to keep everybody in line. More and more people kept arriving.

"I told you there was nothing to worry about," Isaac said. "Almost everybody is here."

"Which means it's time to stop watching and start taking charge," Isaac's mother said. She tried to hand the bullhorn to Isaac.

"Quinn's in charge. Give it to her."

"It's been sanitized," she said as she put it on the ground.

I picked it up with my gloved hand.

"Just push the button and speak."

I brought it up to my lips. "Good evening, everybody!" My words echoed off the houses. I was surprised by how loud my voice was. "Welcome to the Chambers Avenue party! We're so glad you're all here. Thank you for finding your square. We're going to wait a few more minutes for any stragglers to arrive, and then we'll get started."

A gigantic cheer went up.

The first lights came on at the house three doors down. Red and green Christmas lights. Then the house beside it lit up, and then a third and fourth house partway down the block. We'd asked people who lived on the street if they could do that. Many neighbors had. It all looked so beautiful!

I turned to Isaac. "You promised me you're going to play good songs, remember?"

"Quinny, I've made the perfect pandemic playlist. Time to get this party started."

Isaac went to the sound system he'd set up on his driveway. There were wires connected to six speakers spaced along the block. The whole thing had been rented, sanitized and delivered in a police van.

As well, five digital projectors had been set up in sequence along the block. The screens were either a garage door or a sheet strung between step ladders. This was going to be an audio *and* a visual dance.

People had come out of almost every house now, some sitting in lawn chairs, some standing. My mother and father stood at the end of our driveway—six feet apart. I'd drawn two separate squares there just for them. They both gave me a big thumbs-up. On the street, filling every square, were our classmates. Each person wore earbuds, one bud in their ear, the other hanging loose so they could talk to the person in the square facing them. That person was their partner for the first dance. We were ready to go. I gave Isaac the signal.

"Good evening, everyone. Are you ready to party?" Isaac called out clearly through the speakers. In answer, a cheer went up along the street. "Nobody can party like a Panther can party!" There was an even bigger cheer. "I give you our first song of the night!"

The music started playing. I recognized it immediately. It was one my parents liked, an oldie but perfect for the occasion—"Don't Stand So Close to Me," by the Police.

Another cheer went up. It was even louder from the people watching. Kids started dancing. The adults on their driveways started dancing. Their little kids did too. Somehow we'd done it!

Chapter Seventeen

I walked up and down the strip between the rows of squares. Everybody was having a good time. I knew it was partly because we were throwing a great party, but it was more than that. It was like giving somebody a glass of water who'd been wandering in the desert for days with nothing to drink. Everyone was so thirsty for contact with other people—even if that contact was at a distance of six feet and they couldn't touch one another and they were all wearing masks.

And I loved the masks! Some were made from the same material as the dresses. Others had logos from favorite sports teams. Some featured fake smiles and grimaces and even missing teeth. There were monsters, zombies and superheroes. My mask was pretty simple. I was wearing a smile.

Each time a song ended the kid in each square moved one square to their left. It was like a gigantic game of musical chairs except nobody was eliminated. Whoever was in the square across from you was your partner for the next dance. Most of the time everyone was dancing. In fact, there was way more actual dancing than there had ever been at any real school dance.

Sometimes kids took a break. They sat down and had a snack or a drink and talked on the phone to each other. Whether dancing or talking, they were having a good time.

There was a square called Pandemic Pictures, right in front of the Jacobson house. Mr. Jacobson was a really good amateur photographer. He had lots of expensive lenses for his camera and could zoom in from a safe distance to take pictures. He'd also set up a green screen for special effects. We took turns standing in front of the screen, picking a background from anywhere in the world. Maybe we couldn't travel very far right now, but we could look like we were. Kids were placed in front of the pyramids, in Paris, on the moon and under the sea, swimming with turtles and dolphins. The photos were spectacular. I chose the New York City skyline as my background.

These pictures were going to be used for the mask-decorating contest. Miss Fernandez was going to put the pictures on a website, and we would vote for our favorite mask.

Of course, Mr. Jacobson wasn't the only one taking pictures. There had to be thousands and thousands of pictures and videos being taken. Everybody had a phone, and almost everybody had theirs out. There were selfies, shots of other people, videos. I knew everyone would be flooding their social media pages with pictures and videos. Those would be things we could see and remember forever.

In the background of all this was the music. Isaac was *killing* it. He played many different types of songs and got everybody up on their feet.

He played "U Can't Touch This," which I thought was just about the perfect pandemic song. While MC Hammer danced on the screens, I got to see my father do his best imitation of the dance. Turned out my father had some moves.

Isaac had picked lots of the standard guaranteed-to-make-you-want-to-move songs but also a lot that spoke to what this dance was really about. Ones that made us laugh. Or maybe cry a little. Songs like "Don't Stop Believing," "I Think We're Alone Now," "We're All in This Together," "I Will Survive," "The Safety Dance" and "Don't Come Around Here No More."

He was playing—and showing—lots of videos too. When "Renegade" came on, the cheers were so loud I was positive people miles away could have heard the roar. Maybe my father could dance like MC Hammer, but every single person in my class knew the moves to "Renegade." Of course, most of the adults didn't know the song or the dance. Miss Fernandez was an exception.

That was the way it was all night. Different groups reacted or danced to different songs. Isaac seemed to be keeping them all happy. The guy had real DJ skills. And it wasn't just the songs. It was also the things he said between songs, getting people involved, making jokes. It was like all his joking and fooling around in class over the years had prepared him for this.

When the song "Staying Alive" came to an end, Isaac got back on the PA.

"Hey, everyone, I'm afraid to say we're getting close to the end of our night," he announced, and the crowd reacted by booing.

"I know, I know. But we promised to obey the permit laws, and I need you all to help us keep that promise. We do have time for one more song. And it comes with another dedication."

Throughout the night people had been texting Isaac requests.

"This is from Mrs. Reynolds and is dedicated to Mr. Reynolds," he said. A whole bunch of students said, "Oooooh." It made me laugh out loud.

I turned around, looking for our principal. I hadn't known she was even here! I spotted her and her husband standing on one of the driveways. They waved, and people cheered.

"I have to say I'm disappointed Mrs. Reynolds didn't dedicate this to me, since we normally spend so much time together," Isaac said. "But that's okay. Remember, if you don't dance to this one, you're all getting a detention!"

The music started. I watched on the screen as a man with a punky hat climbed out of a garbage can. I knew the song because it was one my parents liked too—"Dancing by Myself." I looked over at Mrs. Reynolds. She and her husband were bouncing up and down to the music. Along the entire block, and on the driveways and grass, it seemed like every single person was dancing. It was magic. And it was nearly over.

Chapter Eighteen

The street was almost empty, and house by house the Christmas lights were being turned off. The screens had been taken down, and the speakers had been returned to Isaac's driveway. At the far end of the street, the last of the police cars drove off. The chalk squares on the street were still there, of course, but there was really not much else left to prove anything had happened. There wasn't even garbage to clean up, since people had taken theirs with them when they left.

I sat down at the edge of my driveway. It was the first time I'd sat down all evening. I closed my eyes and could see the dance playing out in front of me. It made me smile.

"Mind if I join you?"

I looked up. It was my father.

"Of course."

He put his chair down six feet away from me.

"You must be happy," he said.

"Yes. I think it went pretty good."

"Pretty good? It was *amazing*, Quinn. Your mother and I are so proud of you. You did something very important here tonight."

"It was just a dance," I said. "It's not important like what you do."

"Don't underestimate what you did. It was much more than a dance. I don't know how you pulled it off, but for a few hours, during these very strange times, you gave a bunch of people some happiness. You gave them joy. You helped them to forget for a little while. And not just your classmates, but all the people on our street. You gave them hope. You gave *me* hope. Thank you for that. I love you, Q-Cat."

"I love you too, Dad."

"And I'm assuming you both must *really* love me," Isaac called out from his driveway.

I hadn't heard him coming.

"That goes without saying," my father said. "You did an amazing job tonight too, buddy."

"Who would have thought that causing trouble in school would be the perfect training for being a DJ? Although I wasn't able to get Quinn dancing very much."

"I was too busy."

"Are you busy now?" Isaac asked.

"Not really."

"Then you should walk out to the square directly in front of my house."

My father got up from his chair. "I'm going to see how your mom is doing."

"Well?" Isaac asked.

I walked over to the square as Isaac returned to the sound system.

"And our last, last song of the night is dedicated to the person responsible for this whole evening," he said. His voice was quieter but coming through the two speakers that were still hooked up. "For Quinny...the best person I know."

I felt myself blushing.

The music started—"Love at the End of the World."

"I love this song!"

"I know," he said. "That's why I saved it for you."

Isaac walked to the end of the driveway. "Can I have this dance?"

I looked around. "There's nobody else left."

"I know. I didn't want an audience because I'm not much of a dancer," he said.

"I know that too," I said.

He laughed. "You really do keep me honest, Quinny." Isaac started dancing.

He really was bad. And that's what made it so wonderful.

I started dancing too. Somehow I knew it wasn't the end of the world. It was just the start of this dance. It was going to be all right.

Acknowledgments

A book has an author's name on the front. But the creation of a story is always a complex partnership between so many people. With this novel, that was even more true.

Great thanks to an amazing group of beta readers in Florida, Arkansas and places across Canada, for their time, efforts, energy and feedback, which helped shape this book. Thank you, Helen Kubiw, Maddie and Kristen Badger, Luke, Coco and Melanie Mulcaster, Kyla Ross-Day, Fiona Ross, Luke and Stephen Hurley, Kim Moss, Sharon Freeman and, of course, Anita Walters. This book is better because of you.

This book, more than any other I've ever been involved with, was a full team effort from the wonderful Orca "pod." I want to acknowledge and thank designers Rachel Page and Ella Collier;

Susan Adamson and Mark Grill in the production department; Leslie Bootle and her marketing team—Olivia Gutjahr, Kabriya Coghlan, Kennedy Cullen and Michelle Simms van Orden; as well as Naomi Lee, Margaret Bryant and Vivian Sinclair. Special thanks to Tanya Trafford for her input and energy. And finally, Andrew Wooldridge and Ruth Linka, for immediately understanding, accepting and embracing this idea.

I hope this book will entertain, inform, and provide inspiration as we move forward. The future may be unknown, but it is guaranteed.